THIS CANDLEWICK BOOK BELONGS TO:

Text copyright © 1998 by Marjorie Newman
Illustrations copyright © 1998 by Ben Cort

All rights reserved.

First U.S. edition 1998

Library of Congress Cataloging-in-Publication Data is available.

Library of Congress Catalog Card Number 97-12350

ISBN 0-7636-0419-4

2 4 6 8 10 9 7 5 3 1

Printed in Hong Kong

This book was typeset in Bembo Educational.
The pictures were done in colored ink.

Candlewick Press
2067 Massachusetts Avenue
Cambridge, Massachusetts 02140

To Paul
M. N.

To Mum,
Dad, and Ruth
B. C.

HORNPIPE'S HUNT FOR PIRATE GOLD

Marjorie Newman

illustrated by

Ben Cort

CANDLEWICK PRESS
CAMBRIDGE, MASSACHUSETTS

Under this flap and the one on page 23, you'll see lots of extra things to find in the big pictures.

When you have finished reading the story, open out the flaps and start searching!

This is the story of Captain Hornpipe, his pirate crew, and a search for hidden gold.

It all began when his enemy, Crossbones Pete, found a treasure map. Pete's ship had sunk, so he plotted to send the map to Captain Hornpipe—who loved treasure hunts—and then hide on board **his** ship. . . .

The pirates had quite an adventure and needed to solve a lot of puzzles along the way.

Can you help Captain Hornpipe?

- **Read the story and solve the puzzles.**

- **Check your answers at the back when you reach the end, or if you get really stuck.**

Sneakily, Crossbones Pete sent the treasure map to Captain Hornpipe.

Captain Hornpipe guessed Pete was up to no good. But he decided to look for the treasure anyway.

The trouble was that he couldn't make heads or tails of Pete's map.

Can you help Captain Hornpipe figure out where the gold is buried on Grimstone Island?

TREASURE MAP of GRIMSTONE ISLAND

Start by the two crossed trees.

Follow the path between two black rocks.

Go through the trees.

Pass a pond.

Look for the red flowers. We planted them to mark the spot.

To find the gold, you must get there before the flowers die.

Love,
Crossbones Pete

Captain Hornpipe rushed to set sail. But some of the sails were ripped! How would the pirates be able to reach the treasure?

Suddenly Captain Hornpipe remembered the ship belonging to his friend Miranda.

He told Sleepy what Miranda's ship looked like. "Run over and ask Miranda if we can borrow it!" he cried.

But Sleepy wasn't listening carefully!

Can you help him find Miranda's ship? It's the one with a green flag, anchored between a red ship and a black ship.

Miranda agreed to lend them her ship—but only if she could come, too! She knew Captain Hornpipe would say yes.

Captain Hornpipe told his crew to pack—and to hurry! They would catch a bus to the ship.

Oh, dear! Sleepy missed the bus. **Can you help him catch the next one? It must match the bus that Captain Hornpipe is on.**

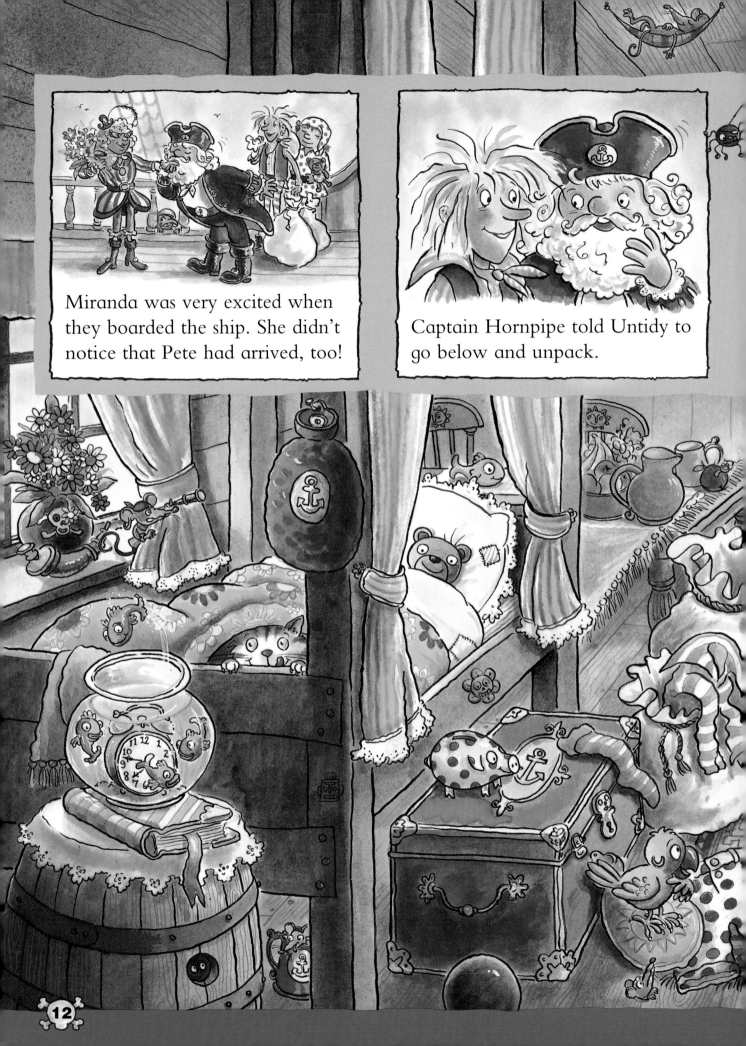

Miranda was very excited when they boarded the ship. She didn't notice that Pete had arrived, too!

Captain Hornpipe told Untidy to go below and unpack.

Untidy was very confused! He, Captain Hornpipe, and Sleepy had each brought five things. But which chests should they go in?

Can you help Untidy? Match the colors and patterns of their things to the labels on the chests.

They set sail, but Captain Hornpipe couldn't figure out which way to go.

Miranda said **she** would figure out the route to Grimstone Island.

"I'll keep watch in case Pete is following us," said Captain Hornpipe. He didn't know that Pete had no ship.

But Miranda couldn't find her glasses. Untidy had put them somewhere and there wasn't time to look for them.

Can you help Miranda pick the best way to go? They mustn't go through whirlpools or past crocodiles.

GRIMSTONE ISLAND

That evening
they ate a huge supper.

Afterward, Captain Hornpipe
went off to steer the ship and
keep a lookout for Pete.

Sleepy and Untidy got ready for bed.

Miranda made up some bedtime riddles about things she could see in the cabin.

Please help Sleepy and Untidy with the answers, or they won't be able to sleep tonight!

What is green, feathery, and has a red beak?

What is cuddly, brown, and furry?

What says "oink" and looks after your money?

What is round and has eight legs?

What has wings and ears and hangs upside down?

The next day the ship sailed straight to Grimstone Island.

They anchored the ship. Then they rowed ashore. Pete watched them all go. . . .

They landed on the island, but couldn't decide which path to take.

Can you help Captain Hornpipe find a safe, clear path up the cliff to the two crossed trees?

They found the treasure!

Sleepy and Untidy took the first load back to the ship. But Pete attacked them and tied them up.

Before Pete fell into the sea . . .

Then Pete went ashore. "I'm taking the treasure **and** your ship," he yelled. "And I'm leaving you two behind on the island."

There was a huge fight! Captain Hornpipe fought well, but it was Miranda who finally won the battle with her rugby tackle. She sent Pete flying into the sea!

Can you see five other things that happened?

and after.

Captain Hornpipe and Miranda
soon rescued Sleepy and Untidy.

And it was Crossbones Pete who
was left behind on the island,
while the others sailed away.

That night they had a party. Captain Hornpipe wished you could have been there to join the fun! During the party they mislaid some of the treasure (and this time it wasn't Untidy's fault!).

 Can you help them find a pearl necklace, a ring, and two gold coins?

Under this flap and the one on page 4, you'll see lots of extra things to find in the big pictures.

When you have finished reading the story, open out the flaps and start searching!

The Answers

- The answers to the story puzzles are shown with single black lines.
- The answers to the fun flap puzzles are shown with double black lines.

Pages 4 and 5

Pages 6 and 7

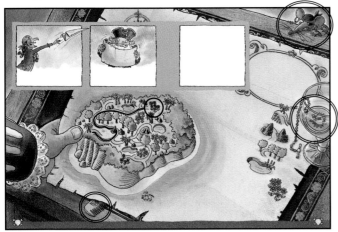

Pages 8 and 9

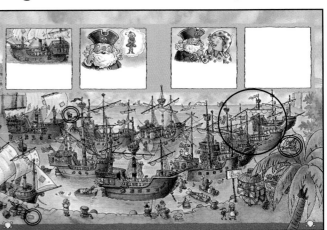

Pages 10 and 11

Pages 12 and 13

Pages 14 and 15

Pages 16 and 17

Pages 18 and 19

Pages 20 and 21

Pages 22 and 23